King Teodoro takes a Queen. Her name is Esperanza.

Madison-Madison Jr. accompanies Princess Tea while she looks for teeth under the pillows of children.

Princess Tea rests after spending so much energy playing.

The King and Court Magician dance a jig. They found the "chant" to help Princess Tea.

Tricionera complains to a policeman that she was not chosen by the King.

LITTLE GRANDMA BOOKS

THE STORY OF
THE SWEET TOOTH FAIRY

Once upon a time in a fairyland far away there were a King and Queen who had a daughter whose name was Teadora. She was named after her father, King Teodoro. Everyone in the Kingdom called her Princess Tea. Princess Tea's mother was the beautiful Queen Esperanza.

Now Princess Tea was a very beautiful child. Her hair and skin were as soft as rose petals and her big, beautiful eyes seemed to be asking, "What is this place and how did I get here?" She was loved by all the people of the Kingdom. Well, almost all of the people.

In this same fairyland in a far corner of the Kingdom, there lived a beautiful woman who had wanted to be chosen by King Teodoro to be his Queen. Her name was Tricionera. She became very angry and very jealous when she was not chosen to be his Queen. She screamed and jumped around like a broken frog. She was miserable and unable to cope with the rejection from the King. She called on her powers to become a witch. So, as you can imagine, she lost some of her beauty.

On the day that Princess Tea was born, Tricionera was there. She hid among the trees and flowers in the Royal Garden until the child was left alone to sleep.

Tricionera then placed a spell on this child of the King.

"You, Princess Tea, will be unable to resist anything sweet to eat. Your teeth will fall out a few days before your sixteenth birthday. We shall see just how pretty you are then. The King and his Queen Esperanza will not be so proud of you then, I'll bet!"

Tricionera laughed and laughed at this cruel joke she had played on King Teodoro and Queen Esperanza. Tricionera was so pleased with herself that she ate three extra bon-bons when she arrived at home.

As the years went by Princess Tea's love for sweets caused a problem for the King and Queen. They feared that her love of sweets would cause her to gain weight, and she would not be healthy. However, her cravings for sugar gave her so much energy that she very seldom sat still. When she was not skipping, she was hopping, jumping or dancing. Most of all Princess Tea loved swimming in the Royal Swimming Pond.

Princess Tea would tire out all the guards, maids, and nurses that were put in charge of her keep. None could keep up with her constant moving about. She would exhaust all of the other children of the Kingdom with her playful games.

As Princess Tea grew older her love for sweets grew as well. On her fifteenth birthday she still would not heed the warnings of the King and Queen.

One day the King was beside himself with worry about Princess Tea's love for sweets. He summoned the Court Magician.

"Madison-Madison", the King bellowed, "we must do something about Princess Tea's love for sweets. She does not seem to outgrow it. We seem unable to get her to even try to eat healthy food. Her mother and I are afraid of what it will do to her figure ..uh..um..that is, her future."

Now Madison-Madison, the Court Magician, was quite old and had become a little more than just a little absent minded. He was forgetful.

"Sire", he replied hastily, and a little sheepishly, "if memory serves me right, there is a magic chant to break habits. I'm afraid that my memory is not serving me right at this very moment. However, if you will allow me a little time, I will try to remember the proper chant. Surely the chant will come back to me!" This last comment was said more under his breath than to the King.

So day after day Madison-Madison walked about the Kingdom with a puzzled look upon his face. With his hands clasped behind his back, his long white beard bobbed up and down as he paced. His old, old eyes drooped in despair. He wanted to do his job well and to please the King.

"After all", he said to himself, "what good is a Court Magician if he cannot perform any magic?"

"Let me see now, how did it go? Frogs sit on logs? Toads who would goad? No. No. That is not right. It seems that it had something to do with small animals. Very small animals. Hmm?"

Suddenly his face brightened up and he smiled out loud.

"Yes! That is it!" he laughed.

"If you crave sweet
For all that you eat,
You must first rub your feet
With the smallest bird you hear tweet!"

"You will find veggies tasty,
 fruits you will crave.
Please don't be too hasty,
about our salads you will rave."

Madison-Madison kept repeating this chant until he reached the Royal Throne Room. Then with a HO! HO! HO! And a click of his pointed shoes, he entered.

"Sire! Oh! Sire!" He exclaimed! "The most wonderful thing has happened. I am beside myself with happiness! I remember! I do! I remember the magic chant to place on the Royal Princess to help her to like vegetables and other healthy foods!"

Now it was the King who was beside himself with excitement. The King and the Court Magician began to dance a jig. In all their excitement they had not noticed the presence of Queen Esperanza.

"Please! Please?!" The Queen pleaded with them. "Will you please stop this ridiculous dancing and prancing about? What does this have to do with the Princess? Why have you kept this from me?"

"My dear", said the King, huffing and puffing and looking for his throne to fall into. "We did not want to worry you about this. That is why Madison-Madison and I kept it a secret from you. It must, at all cost, remain the secret of the three of us!"

The King and Madison-Madison explained what they had planned in order to help the Royal Princess.

The Queen, who was usually very prim and proper, shouted "Yiiipppeeee", in her shrillest voice. Then, much to the astonishment of the Court Magician and the King, she did a triple twirl before landing, quite clumsily, on the lap of the King. The King laughed. "Esp-pey, please, we are not alone here", he said in his playful voice.

The Queen then hastily stood-up, cleared her throat, rearranged her crown and smoothed her royal dress. In her calmest voice with her head held high she stated, "Not a peep of what happened here today shall be discussed outside of this room! Or in fact, inside of this room!"

The Queen left the King and Madison-Madison alone to plan their next move.

The very next day Princess Tea was in the Royal Garden. She had been playing and lay to rest. She fell asleep and her crown and shoes had fallen off. They were on the ground under her shaded Mosaic bench. Madison-Madison was nearby and awoke her to talk with her. He asked her if she had noticed all the beautiful birds in the garden that morning. She nodded yes and smiled at the Court Magician.

"Have you seen the littlest bird, Princess Tea? It sings beautifully to you. I will bring it closer so that you may hear it better." Then Madison-Madison placed a spell on the littlest bird and brought it to the Royal Princess.

"Oh, thank you!" said the Royal Princess. "I will hold it for a while."

While Princess Tea held the little bird, Madison-Madison placed a spell on her. Then while she was under his spell and sitting quite still, he helped her rub her feet with the softness of the smallest bird.

When they finished rubbing the feet of the Princess, Madison-Madison released her and the smallest bird from the spell he had placed on them.

The deed was done!

Madison-Madison was quite pleased with himself when, in the Royal Dining Room that evening, he was able to give the King the "thumbs up" signal. This was the sign to the King that the deed had been accomplished. The King returned the signal and then winked at the Queen.

The next day Princess Tea tasted her first vegetable salad and exclaimed "Oh, my! What a clean and refreshing taste. I had no idea vegetables tasted so good." The King and Queen were delighted to see this at long last.

A few months later, just a few days before Princess Tea's sixteenth birthday, something awful happened. All of her teeth fell out! The spell that Tricionera had placed on Princess Tea had now come true.

The whole Kingdom was in an uproar! The Queen collapsed and the King was in a furor and screaming for Madison-Madison.

Tricionera, the witch, was very happy when she came to hide in the Royal Garden. She watched the unhappiness she caused by the spell she had placed on the Royal Princess.

Now Tricionera had not seen anyone in the Royal Garden while she was laughing, but Madison-Madison Jr. had been playing there. He ran to hide when he saw Tricionera approaching. He had never seen her before.

Tricionera laughed and laughed and carelessly said aloud, "Aha! So my spell works and the Royal Princess loses her teeth. It has certainly been worth waiting for. Let us see just how happy the Royal Couple will be now!"

Madison-Madison Jr. ran to find his father to tell him what he had seen and heard in the Royal Garden.

The poor Court Magician on hearing these words from his son understood exactly what had befallen their beautiful Royal Princess. The whole Kingdom had thought that the Princess's love for sweets was her own love for sweets. They didn't know that Tricionera had placed such an evil, awful and terrible curse on their Princess.

Well he would certainly not rest until Tricionera had a taste of her own ugliness. His powers grew stronger with each moment of anger.

The Court Magician grew angrier and angrier. He removed all Tricionera's powers. Then he placed a spell on her for all her hair and all her teeth to fall out. The whole Kingdom watched in disbelief. Tricionera was astounded and raged at the Court Magician. It was not a pretty sight.

It took four of the King's strongest guards to remove Tricionera from the Kingdom. She was taken to a deserted island to live alone forever.

In the meantime, Princess Tea was so embarrassed that she could not be persuaded to leave her bedroom. She had not eaten a morsel in days.

The King and Queen could not be comforted. They felt that they had failed as parents. "What good is being the King and the Queen if we cannot help our own Princess?" cried the Queen.

On Princess Tea's sixteenth birthday there was much sadness in the Kingdom. The King and Queen were locked in the Royal Throne Room trying to console each other. The Royal Princess would not see them, or anyone else for that matter.

Madison-Madison Sr. paced up and down trying to think of a way to make everyone happy once again.

Madison-Madison Jr. said to his father, "I wish I had magical powers. If I could, I would give Princess Tea all the teeth in the world so she would be happy again."

"What a wonderful idea, son!" said Madison-Madison Sr. "Of course! I'll give Princess Tea a gift for her birthday. She will be able to have all the teeth that she will ever need!"

Now Madison-Madison Sr. had undone the spell that Tricionera had placed on Princess Tea of eating sweets. But he had not undone the spell in time to keep Princess Tea's teeth from falling out. However, he was able to do the next best thing if the Royal Princess would allow him to.

Princess Tea gratefully accepted this wonderful gift from the Court Magician. He gave her the ability to search for teeth under the pillows of growing children.

As the mortal children grow they "lose" each "baby" tooth, which is then replaced by a permanent tooth. One by one as each tooth falls out the child places it under his or her pillow at night. In the calmness of the night the beautiful "Sweet Tooth" Fairy, Princess Tea, collects the teeth she needs and leaves a small gift for the child.

That is how Princess Tea became the Sweet-Tooth Fairy, thanks to Madison-Madison, Sr. and his son Madison-Madison Jr.

King Teodoro and Queen Esperanza were glad to see Princess Tea happy again.

Even though the Princess has to gather teeth from mortal children forever, she is grateful for the gift. She is accompanied by Madison-Madison Jr. who watches over her while she gathers the teeth.

And they lived happily ever after. The Sweet Tooth Fairy able to gather beautiful teeth. The King and Queen having a happy daughter again. Madison-Madison Sr. feeling good about solving the Royal Family problems. Madison-Madison Jr. having the important job of accompanying Princess Tea on her journeys to gather the teeth.

The Sweet Tooth Fairy
In
Pictures

This is the Royal Throne Room where the important decisions of the Kingdom are discussed and important decisions are made. The Royal Guards are guarding the palace property and protecting the Royal Family.

The King has invited Esperanza, a maiden from the Royal Kingdom, to accompany him at the Royal Palace for the evening. They are in the Royal Flower Garden Gazebo in front of the Royal Throne Room.

This picture shows King Teodoro proposing to the beautiful Esperanza. He is asking her to be his wife, his queen and his companion forever.

Now Esperanza had been hoping and praying that King Teodoro would ask her father for her hand in marriage. She knew King Teodoro would not ask her to marry him unless he had the approval of her father. Esperanza was so happy to know that had all been settled.

She said "yes".

Tricionera was another beautiful maiden from the Royal Kingdom. She was told by her brother that the King had chosen Esperanza to become his queen. Tricionera's heart was broken. Tricionera jumped around like a broken frog. Then she jumped up on a bench at the Royal Park Zoo and yelled at everyone that walked by.

Then, as if that was not enough action to show her anger, she went to the FAIRY POLICE! They were so shocked that they closed down the Royal Police Department. They had to study the rules. Were there any such rules or laws pertaining to being "rejected" or "not chosen" by the King? (I don't think so!?)

Oh! Me! How would the Chief of Police handle such a case? This was not good!

The worst action Tricionera took was when the Town Criers were announcing the wedding date in the streets. She tried to stop them. She stood right in front of them as they were trying to cry out the news. She waved her arms and legs and said very unkind things to them, or rather, at them.

She was not happy.

At last the Royal Wedding Day was here. The wedding was in the Royal Courtyard where the benches were set up for the guests. Everyone seemed happy and contented that the wedding would be family oriented and a pleasant time for everyone.

There was plenty of delicious food prepared by the Royal Chefs. Every woman in the Kingdom had baked her own "specialty dessert" to take to the reception. It was a tradition that they shared down through the years. These desserts had become a favorite part of the wedding celebration.

The King and his bride were very happy to share this special time with everyone. Queen Esperanza's family was there and they were glad to be part of her past and her future. They knew that the King was a good King, beloved and respected by the people.

Their Esperanza was in good hands and everyone was happy.

The arrival of the Royal Child was full of anticipation a year later. Queen Esperanza sat on the balcony outside the Royal Palace. As the time for the birth of the Royal Child approached, she became more excited. Everyone was very excited. The Royal Doctor was with the Queen at the first sign of the Royal Birth. She was ready.

Soon it was announced that a Royal Princess had been born. Everyone cheered. After everyone had seen the Princess, she was placed under a tree in the Royal Garden to take a nap in the clean afternoon air.

No one noticed a dark figure hiding under the bushes and flowers in the Royal Garden. When everyone was gone, Tricionera came out of her hiding place. She glared at the baby. She placed a wicked spell on the child of the King and Queen. Tricionera was still very angry at not being selected to be the queen of their Fairyland. "Now we'll just wait and see", she said to herself.

Princess Tea was full of energy most of the time. Just eating a lot of sweets gave her so much energy that she could beat anyone at the fastest games that anyone could come up with.

She was an excellent dancer, rope jumper, relay runner, swimmer and any other sport that required a lot of physical energy. She was tireless and she always seemed to be happy.

The children of the Kingdom loved her and were so happy to have her as a friend. She was everyone's friend and enjoyed all out door games as well as games of Hide and Seek. This game was a favorite of the children. The children were always welcome in the spacious Royal Palace. When it was Princess Tea's turn to be "it" and look for the others, she would giggle and try to be keen and swift to catch them.

When Princess Tea turned fifteen years of age, the King and Queen were really worried about her and her love of sweets.

The King called the Royal Magician. The Magician was indeed concerned that nothing was helping the Princess to learn the value of fruits and vegetables in her diet.

The Court Magician remembered an old chant that would help the Princess to try to eat well.

The Court Magician presented his plan to King Teodoro to help the Princess with her diet. They were so happy that they danced a jig.

When Princess Tea began to eat a better diet it made everyone happy.

One day Princess Tea was in the Royal Garden listening to the birds and other little animals play and sing.

After she fell asleep on her Mosaic bench, the Court Magician awoke her and placed a spell on her. He captured the smallest bird and, using the "chant", he helped her rub her feet with the small bird. This "chant" changed her taste so that she liked to eat healthy food.

King Teodoro and Queen Esperanza were happy to hear how Madison-Madison had been able to help Princess Tea.

It looked as if the Princess would continue to eat foods that were healthy as well as good tasting. The Royal Chefs were trying very hard to prepare dishes that would please Princess Tea.

Everything went well until the evil spell that had been placed on the Royal Princess at birth came true. No one could have guessed that Princess Tea's love of sweets all those years was a curse. It was thought to be her natural desire for sugar.

And they lived happily ever after. The Sweet Tooth Fairy able to gather beautiful teeth. The King and Queen having a happy daughter again. Madison-Madison Sr. feeling good about solving the Royal Family problems. Madison-Madison Jr. having the important job of accompanying Princess Tea on her journeys to gather the teeth.

King Teodoro takes a Queen. Her name is Esperanza.

Madison-Madison Jr. accompanies Princess Tea while she looks for teeth under the pillows of children.

Princess Tea rests after spending so much energy playing.

The King and Court Magician dance a jig. They found the "chant" to help Princess Tea.

Tricionera complains to a policeman that she was not chosen by the King.

THE END

About Little Grandma, "Abuelita"

 Little Grandma was born and raised in rural New Mexico. When she was young she chopped wood for the cook stove, and pumped water from the outside well for cooking, bathing, and cleaning. She rode bareback on the neighbor's horse, and picked wild spinach and asparagus from the ditch banks. She swam in the muddy Rio Grande River and played Tarzan in the cottonwood trees.

Little Grandma currently enjoys music, old movies, hiking, painting and writing poems. She is grateful for the blessings God has given her with family and loved ones.

LITTLE GRANDMA BOOKS

www.ingramcontent.com/pod-product-compliance
Lightning Source LLC
Chambersburg PA
CBHW041006170626
46815CB00002B/185